ZONDERKIDZ

The Friendly Beasts
Copyright © 2012 by Zondervan
Illustrations © 2012 by Anna Vojtech

Requests for information should be addressed to:

Zonderkidz, 5300 Patterson Ave. SE, *Grand Rapids, Michigan 49530*

Library of Congress Cataloging-in-Publication Data

The friendly beasts; an old English Christmas carol / illustrated by Anna Vojtech.
     p. cm.
    ISBN 978-0-310-72012-6 (hardcover)
  1. Carols, English—England—Texts. 2. Christmas music—Texts. 3. Folk songs, English—
England—Texts. [1. Carols. 2. Christmas music. 3. Folk songs.] I. Vojtech, Anna, ill.
PZ8.3.F91168 2011
782.28'1723—dc22
[E]   2010018739

Published in association with the literary agency of Alive Comunications, Inc., 7680 Goddard Street, Suite 200, Colorado Springs, CO 80920, www.alivecommunications.com

Zonderkidz is a trademark of Zondervan.

Editor: Barbara Herndon
Art direction & design: Cindy Davis

Printed in China

12 13 14 15 16 17 /LPC/ 6 5 4 3 2 1

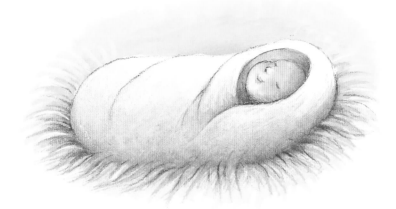

For Cyrus
—A.V.

To Lexi Rivers—the coolest kid I know!
Keep living your life for Jesus, sweet girl.
Aunt Bec loves you.
—R.S.J.

PERFORMED AND NARRATED BY **REBECCA ST. JAMES**

The Friendly Beasts

Illustrations by
Anna Vojtech

ZONDERkidz

ZONDERVAN.com/
AUTHORTRACKER
follow your favorite authors

Jesus, our Brother, kind and good,

was humbly born in a stable rude.

And the friendly beasts around him stood,

Jesus, our Brother, kind and good.

"I," said the donkey, shaggy and brown,

"I carried his mother up hill and down;

I carried her safely to Bethlehem Town."
"I," said the donkey, shaggy and brown.

"I," said the cow, all white and red,
"I gave him my manger for a bed;

I gave him my hay to pillow his head."
"I," said the cow, all white and red.

15

"I," said the sheep with curly horn,
"I gave him my wool for his blanket warm;

He wore my coat on Christmas morn."

"I," said the sheep with curly horn.

"I," said the camel, yellow and black,
"over the desert upon my back,

I brought him a gift in the wise man's pack."
"I," said the camel, yellow and black.

"I," said the dove from the rafters high,
"cooed him to sleep that he should not cry.

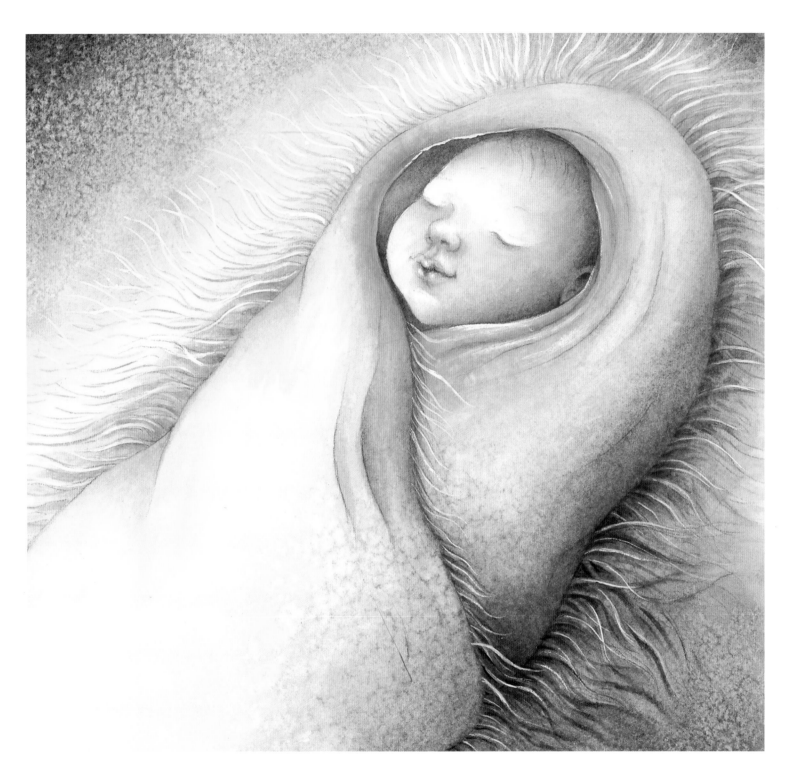

We cooed him to sleep, my mate and I."
"I," said the dove from the rafters high.

Thus every beast by some good spell,

in the stable dark was glad to tell,

of the gift he gave Emmanuel.

The gift he gave Emmanuel.

The Friendly Beasts

Traditional

1. Je - sus, our Broth - er, kind and good, was
2. "I," said the don - key, shag - gy and brown, "I
3. "I," said the cow, all white and red, "I

hum - bly born in a sta - ble rude. And the
car - ried his moth - er up hill and down; I
gave him my man - ger for a bed; I

friend - ly   beasts   a - round   him   stood,
car - ried   her   safe - ly   to   Beth - le - hem   Town."
gave him   my   hay   to   pil - low   his   head."

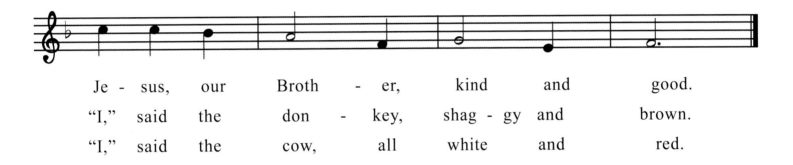

Je - sus,   our   Broth - er,   kind   and   good.
"I,"   said   the   don - key,   shag - gy   and   brown.
"I,"   said   the   cow,   all   white   and   red.

4. "I," said the sheep with curly horn,
   "I gave him my wool for his blanket warm;
   He wore my coat on Christmas morn."
   "I," said the sheep with curly horn.

5. "I," said the camel, yellow and black,
   "over the desert upon my back,
   I brought him a gift in the wise man's pack."
   "I," said the camel, yellow and black.

6. "I," said the dove from the rafters high,
   "cooed him to sleep that he should not cry.
   We cooed him to sleep, my mate and I."
   "I," said the dove from the rafters high.

7. Thus every beast by some good spell,
   in the stable dark was glad to tell
   of the gift he gave Emmanuel.
   The gift he gave Emmanuel.